Scholastic
CLIFFORD
THE BIG RED DOG

Phonics Fun
Reading Program — Book 5: u

The Small Red Puppy

by Grace Maccarone

Illustrated by John Kurtz

Based on the books by Norman Bridwell

SCHOLASTIC INC.
New York   Toronto   London   Auckland   Sydney
Mexico City   New Delhi   Hong Kong   Buenos Aires

Emily Elizabeth had
a puppy.

His name was Clifford.

Clifford the puppy was
very, very small.

He was smaller than
a toy.

But he was a real dog.

"You are too small," she said.

"I hope you grow.

But I love you even if you are small."

She gave him a hug.

Clifford loved
Emily Elizabeth, too.

Clifford the puppy
grew up . . .

and up . . .

and up!

"You are very, very big now!

You can stop," said Emily Elizabeth.

And he did!